The Mud Baby

Shanta Rameshwar Rao

Illustrated by Taposhi Ghoshal

Orient BlackSwan

The river was flowing gently along,
The breeze was waiting, humming its song,
The frogs in the water had ceased to hop–
Their games and croaking had come to a stop.

Yes, everyone was waiting without a sound,
'Will she come?' asked an ant from her hole in the ground.
'Of course she will!' promised a young water rat;
'She will, she will,' murmured an upside-down bat.

Then suddenly a bird sang out loud and clear,
'There she is! There she is! She's drawing near!'
And so she was–down the path she came...
'Parvati,' they whispered, for that was her name.

In the cool river water Parvati stood
Laughing: 'Oh this water! It feels so good!'
She splashed, and she splished without a care,
And the fishes all laughed and leapt in the air.

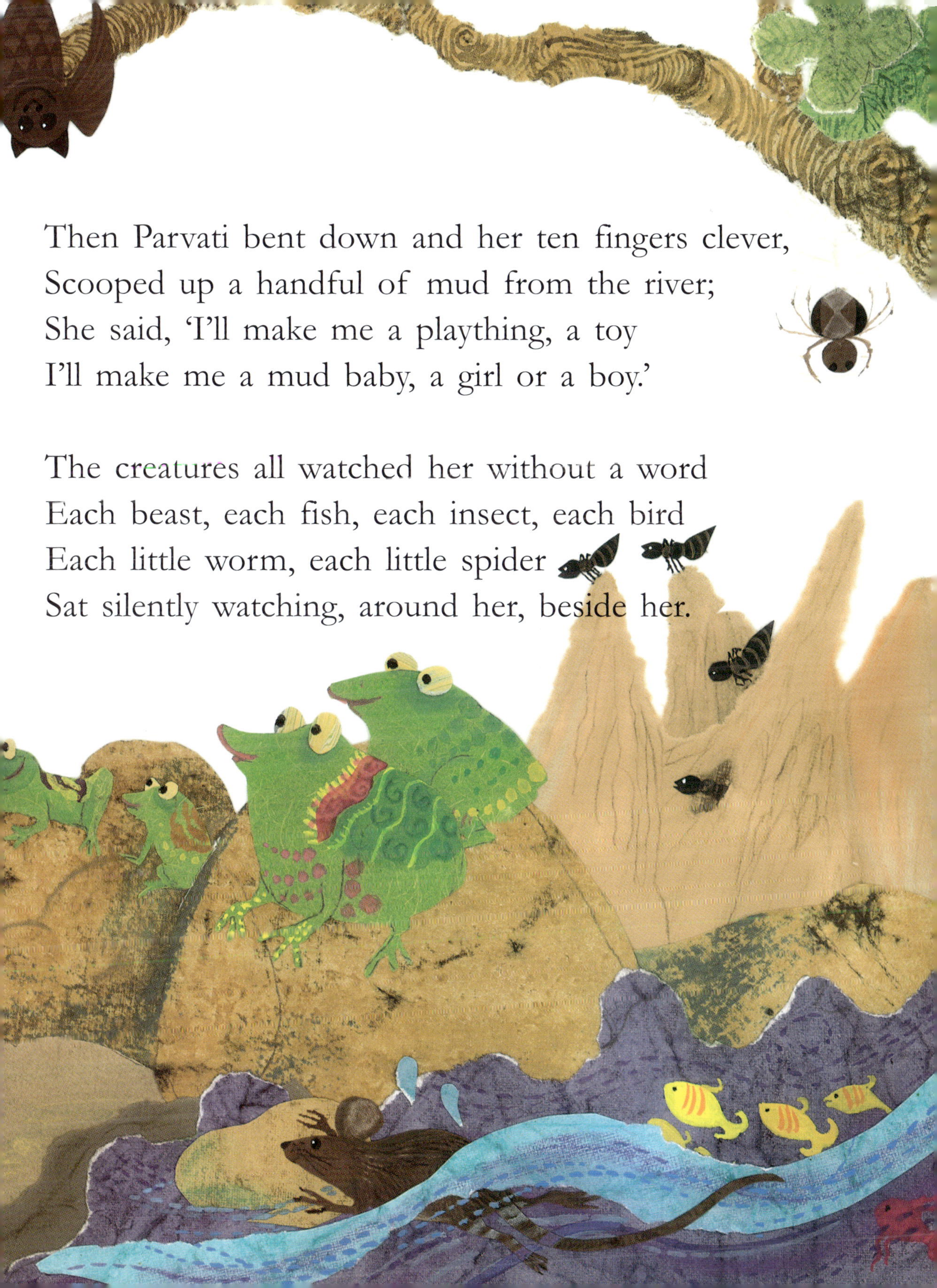

Then Parvati bent down and her ten fingers clever,
Scooped up a handful of mud from the river;
She said, 'I'll make me a plaything, a toy
I'll make me a mud baby, a girl or a boy.'

The creatures all watched her without a word
Each beast, each fish, each insect, each bird
Each little worm, each little spider
Sat silently watching, around her, beside her.

'First I'll roll out this lump of mud,' she said,
'And from it make a nice round little head.'
Then with a turn of her wrist, fingers and thumb
She shaped a mud body, podgy and plump.

Then Parvati's forefinger went dum-diddle-diddle
And lo! right there in the mud baby's middle
A round belly button like a full moon appeared
And everyone laughed and everyone cheered.

Arms and legs, fingers and toes–
But 'Oh!' laughed Parvati, 'I've forgotten his nose!'
So she gave him a nose and she gave him a chin
And dimples where smiles went out and in.

And two ears, one on each side of his head,
'And now for two bottoms,' Parvati said;
She shaped those with care and he was complete
From the curly hair on his head to the soles of his feet.

She laid him down on the rock where she sat,
And he lay there unmoving, silent and fat;
He did not gurgle when she tickled his tummy,
Nor open his mouth to call out, 'Mummy! Mummy!'

Sighed Parvati, 'Oh my son, made of brown river mud,
How I wish you were real, made of flesh and red blood!
I wish you would not lie still, like a mud lump
I wish, my darling, you'd stand up and jump.'

The words had hardly escaped from her mouth
When lights shone from east, from west, north and south.
And the mud baby leapt up crying, 'Mummy! Mummy!
Tickle me, tickle me, tickle my tummy!'

He skipped and jumped and fell on his face
And scampered about, wouldn't stay in one place.
The creatures around let out a great shout:
'Oh what joy to see him running about!'

'Ganesha,' they called him, Parvati's wish had come true–
Her plump mud baby came alive, and grew
Into a dear little boy who loved to eat
Goodies, especially things that were sweet.

Like modaks stuffed with raisins and spice,
Laddoos, jalebis, pedhas and sweet rice
Glistening with syrup and pink sugar ice,
He finished them all in a trice.

And all the goodies, whether cold or hot
To share them with others he never forgot.
So everyone loved him for his generous ways
And sang to him songs of welcome and praise.